The Kid with TOO Many PETS

written and illustrated
by Harland Williams

PSS!
PRICE STERN SLOAN

For Ann O'Sullivan–H.W.

Text and illustrations © 2004 by Harland Williams. All rights reserved. Published by Price Stern Sloan, a division of Penguin Young Readers Group, 345 Hudson Street, New York, New York 10014. *PSS!* is a trademark of Penguin Group (USA) Inc. Manufactured in China.

Library of Congress Cataloging-in-Publication Data

Williams, Harland, 1962-
  The kid with too many pets / written and illustrated by Harland Williams.
    p. cm.
  Summary: An unusual boy has filled his house with elephants, giraffes, and hundreds of other pets, much to the dismay of his father and the townspeople, but when he tries to add just one more animal, everyone is in for a big surprise.
  ISBN 0-8431-1010-4 (hardcover)
  [1. Pets–Fiction. 2. Animals–Fiction. 3. Stories in rhyme.] I. Title.

PZ8.3.W6775Ki 2004
  [E]–dc22
  ISBN 0-8431-1010-4
  1 3 5 7 9 10 8 6 4 2

2003022540

This is the story of a rather strange kid.

In fact, it's quite possible that he flipped his lid.

He liked to keep pets, as most of us do,

But can you believe he had
five-hundred-and-two?

The kitchen had an elephant, and a polar bear with cubs.

The bathroom was full of hippos hanging out in the tub.

A whole herd of mountain goats lived on the stairs.
While the family room was full of lions snoring in chairs.

In the bedroom, there was a rhino with a toy on his horn,
And in the bed some orangutans eating popcorn.

I could go on forever, but I have to slow down
And tell you a bit about the rest of the town.
The whole community was upset, to say the least—
The neighbors, the mayor, and even the priest!

For they had no pets—the kid had them all,
They had no cat to stroke and no dog to call.
So they all got together to have a protest
To demand that this kid start to share with the rest.

And as fate would have it, on that same day in June,
Father came home for lunch at exactly twelve noon.
When he opened the front door, OH, DON'T YOU KNOW?
He got a big, soggy kiss from a water buffalo.

Father pushed his way in and cleared a path to the couch
Where a crazy kangaroo was planting flowers in her pouch.

The den was being used by some laughing hyenas,
And a whole herd of giraffes looking for Kenya.

"That's it!" Father shouted. "I can't take any more!"
He threw on his hat and ran back out the door.
And not even a second after he stepped off the front mat,
He discovered a three-toed sloth stuck to his back.
"It's over!" he hollered as he turned to his son.
"No more pets, do you hear me? Not even ONE!"

The kid couldn't believe it. He sat and he frowned.
Then something moved near his feet on the ground.
It was small, brown, and bumpy and looked like a frog.
He thought, *I don't have a pet that looks quite this odd.*

I just have to have it. What's one more pet going to hurt?
He bent down and grabbed it and hid it under his shirt.
He snuck to the mail slot and stuffed in the toad.
And do you know what happened?

It caused the roof to explode!

There wasn't enough room. Father was right.
Now the kid hoped that his dad wasn't coming home tonight.
But it was too late, the damage was done,
The sky was full of animals flying high toward the sun.

They flew miles high, past the clouds and a plane.
It was quite a strange sight—it was rather insane!
But like that old line, "What goes up must come down . . ."
Down they did come—all over the town!

They came in through walls and windows and roofs.
A porcupine in a man's lap while they filled in his tooth.

Another man in his kitchen, enjoying some soup,
Was suddenly joined by a large, black bear group.

Imagine waking up to this kind of surprise—
A huge feathered ostrich staring right in your eyes!

And what about an alligator landing inside your car,
It wouldn't be smart to drive very far!
But at least all of the townsfolk were getting a pet,
There was no more reason for them to be all upset.

Even Father was pleased when he got home that night
To find the house empty—not one pet in sight!
Finally, he could relax now that the rooms were all bare,
Though he still did not know that the roof was not there.

And what about the kid? Well, that's not hard to explain.
He's busy outside starting his collection again.